acknowledgments

Many thanks to the Blue Chair, Shenanigans, and the Lemon Fair, whose goodies and goods dance in children's heads and serve as stocking stuffers. I'm grateful for the late Gay Alvarez, Lemon Fair founder, who gave Sewanee angels a place to spread their wings and fly. The Lemon Fair angels led me to the talented Christi Teasley, who masterfully illustrated this little book. Thank you to Gerald Smith, recently retired Sewanee religion professor whose 47-year career exemplifies what makes this place special and unique. Finally, Christi and I couldn't have done this without the superb art direction/design of Laura Deleot (C '96) and Circa Design.

The Sewanee Night Before Christmas

Copyright ©2018 Katie Hines Porterfield
www.atozchildrensbooks.com

Art by Christi Teasley
Art Direction and Book Design by Circa Design

Printed in the United States

www.mascotbooks.com

For more information, please contact:
Mascot Books
620 Herndon Parkway, Suite 320
Herndon, VA 20170
info@mascotbooks.com

Library of Congress Control Number:
2017915773

CPSIA Code: PBANG1117A
ISBN-13: 978-1-68401-679-2

To Forrest, my best friend and favorite
Sewanee grad, and Hines and Shep,
my favorite little editors.

The Sewanee
Night Before Christmas

Katie Hines Porterfield

ART BY CHRISTI TEASLEY

'Twas the night before Christmas
in Sewanee, Tennessee,
not a student was stirring—
they'd gone home, you see.

Their gowns were hung in their closets with care,
awaiting the semester that would soon be there.

Professors' kids were nestled
all snug in their beds,
while visions of Blue Chair treats
danced in their heads.

And Ma in her soccer sweats,
and I in my alumni apparel,
were discussing the magic
of each *Lesson and Carol.*

When out on the Quad
we heard a strange noise,
it was louder than a group of wild frat boys.
Away to the window I ran with a frown,
knocking over my senior year
"Cap and Gown."

The moon above All Saints lit up the whole sky,
and I was glad the fog had yet to stop by.

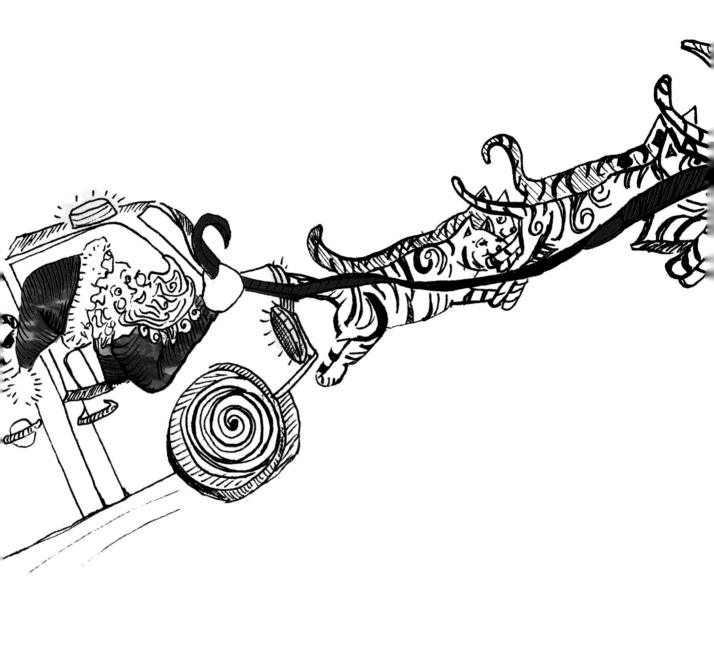

When what to my wondering eyes did I spot,
but St. Nick with the reins of eight tigers taut.
The tigers flew Bacchus right through the air,
and I heard Santa say, "Head over there!"
He pointed to my house, and how quickly they came,
as he was barely able to get out each name.
"Now Hunter, now Elliott, now Benedict and Johnson!
On Cannon, on Trezevant, and on Hoffman and Hodgson!"

"To the top of Breslin, over the only light in town!

Now here we are—to the roof, let's touch down!"

I ran downstairs and peeked from
behind a door,
He stepped from the chimney,
placing his sack on the floor.

He had Sewanee purple flair
and white hair like G. Smith,
and he was jolly and plump
just like in the myth.

With rosy cheeks and dimples, he was super cute,
and he filled our stockings with _Lemon Fair_ loot.
There were angel mugs and posters and stickers, too,
even a gift card for _Shenanigans_ — woo-hoo!

He spoke not a word until he finished his work,
and then gave me a smile and turned with a jerk.
"Ecce Quam Bonum," he said, laying finger to nose,
and with a proud nod, up the chimney he rose.

He whistled like the coach of those "Iron Men" greats,
and away his team flew like angels fleeing the gates.
But I heard him exclaim as he drove out of sight,

"Merry Christmas to all, and Yea Sewanee's Right!

The End

author KATIE HINES PORTERFIELD

A writer based in Nashville, Tennessee, Katie Hines Porterfield graduated from the University of the South in 1998. In 2014, she wrote and published *Sewanee A to Z* to share the magic of the "Mountain" with her twin boys. Katie is also the author of *Find Your Heart in Lake Martin,* an A to Z book about another place close to her heart. In addition to her B.A. in American Studies, she holds an M.A. in journalism from the University of Alabama. See her work and purchase books at atozchildrensbooks.com.

artist CHRISTI TEASLEY

Christi Teasley lives in Monteagle, Tennessee, with her husband, Carlton Young. Christi attended St. Andrew's School, Sewanee Academy, and the merged St. Andrew's-Sewanee School from which she graduated in 1983. She received a B.F.A. in Textiles and an M.A. in Art Education from the Rhode Island School of Design. She returned to the "Mountain" and taught visual art at St. Andrew's-Sewanee School from 1989-2016. Christi's studio practice includes drawing, painting, dyeing, printing, and stitching.

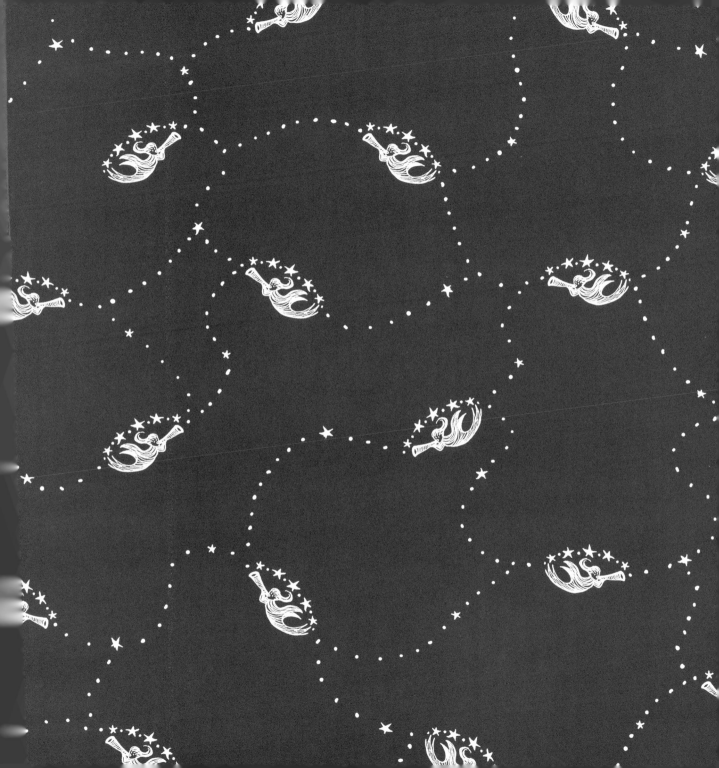